Magical Mayhem

Prologue
To Prevent First Place

Emily Martha Sorensen

Also by Emily Martha Sorensen

Standalones:
Black Magic Academy

Fairy Senses:
Fairy Eyeglasses
Fairy Compass
Fairy Earmuffs
Fairy Barometer
Fairy Pox
Fairy Slippers
Fairy Lunchbox
Fairy Icepack
Fairy Stopwatch
Fairy Toothbrush
Fairy Perfume

Dragon Eggs:
Dragon's Egg
Dragon's Hope
Dragon's First Christmas
Dragon's Fire

Comics:
A Magical Roommate
To Prevent World Peace

Picture Books:
Tabby, Tabby, Burning Bright

The End in the Beginning:
The Keeper and the Rulership
The Fires of the Rulership
The Magic or the Rulership

Trilogy of a Teenage Werevulture:
Trials of a Teenage Werevulture
Trifles of a Teenage Werevulture
Weredodo Sleuth

The Numbers Just Keep
Getting Bigger:
Twenty-Four Potential
Children of Prophecy

Not Quite a Harem:
Not Quite a Curse

Magical Mayhem:
To Prevent World Peace
To Prevent Chic Costumes
To Prevent Clear Paths
To Prevent Smart Choices
To Prevent Warm Welcomes
To Prevent Cute Mascots

Short Story Collections:
Worlds of Wonder
Magic and Mischief

To Prevent First Place

To Frederik Vendelin,

longtime fan of the comic,
reader of my other books,
and Patreon supporter.

Chapter 1
The Enemy

Overall, Kendra was not a very patient person. Not even when she was her alter ego, Cream Angel.

Make that *especially* when she was her alter ego, Cream Angel.

"Green Fairy, pick a flower and stick with it!" Kendra shouted, ducking under the leg of a ceramic minion that was trying, for some reason, to kick her in the face.

Felicity had been dithering between lilacs and buttercups for nearly ten seconds, while Florence had been breathing fire in a ring around her to keep out the ceramic minions. Dithering in the middle of a battle was the opposite of helpful.

"I've got it!" Felicity cried, uprooting a buttercup from the flower patch she had been examining. "This one!"

Florence didn't wait for anything further. She wheeled around and breathed a stream of fire through three minions that had unwisely stood in a row outside the fire ring. All three disintegrated to ash immediately.

"Bind them!" Felicity cried. The buttercup's roots shot out and wrapped around two more minions that had been standing nearby, covering them with shoots and yellow flowers as the roots dug into the minions' skin. Against humans, that would have been horrifying, but against ceramic, it was merely useful to watch the fragile minions crack into useless rubble.

Kendra didn't stop to watch for longer than a split second. She snatched the halo from where it was hovering over her head, flung it outward at her target, and it knocked one minion sprawling into another. The two impact was so violent that the two smashed, cracking one severely and making the other crumble.

The cracked one came racing back at Kendra. If there had been a face on that smooth ceramic head, it would have had its teeth gritted in sheer determination.

Whoosh! The halo returned to Kendra's hand in an arc like a boomerang. She flung it forward again.

Wham! The cracked minion was knocked off its feet.

Florence ran past her, breathing fire every which way.

"Bind! Bind! Bind!" Felicity was shouting.

Kendra tossed the halo over her head to have it hover in case she needed it, and flapped her large, white feathered wings. She rose up in the air, surveying the battlefield around them.

Ridiculous. There have to be about two hundred minions!

In many ways, their third arch-nemesis was less annoying than their first two had been. The drug lord they'd initially fought had had an army of lawyers to protect him against going to prison, no matter how many times they'd caught him, and their second . . . well, the less said about Dark Deathwave and his son, a.k.a. the jerk who had turned out to be Florence's boyfriend and nearly tempted her to the side of evil, the better.

But Queen Hemlock had one little, tiny thing about her that was extremely maddening: namely, the fact that she wasn't limited to minions she could hire. She could *make* them. A seemingly limitless supply of these ceramic minions, in fact.

Oh, it wasn't like they were as strong as people. They were also much stupider. And you could kill them without worrying that some kid would never see their dad again.

But on the other hand, these battles with faceless ceramic were simultaneously really dull and much more terrifying. Wars of attrition were *not* the reason Kendra had become a magical girl, and *not* the way she wanted to be fighting. She wanted to be ending evil plans, not holding off baked dirt every week.

Something caught Kendra's eye. She dove, snapping her wings and and diving down with the speed of a fierce bird of prey. Her target was there, the one who had brought those stupid ceramics with her. If she could just reach before —

The target looked up and spied Kendra diving. In a flash, the girl with four braids had dropped, leaving Kendra with no choice but to snatch the branch the villain had just been on in order to grab it, swing around, and use her momentum to shoot off in the next direction.

Nightshade, Princess of Poison, saw her coming. She leapt in the air and then disappeared.

Kendra roared with rage. She was so sick of losing Queen Hemlock's lackey that way, she could just scream. In fact, she was going to! She flapped upwards and yelled with fury.

"Not very angelic," Felicity giggled from beside her.

Kendra's eyes opened, and she looked over at her teammate. Translucent green butterfly wings flapping behind her, Felicity was hovering next to her.

"Aren't you supposed to be killing ceramic?" Kendra asked sourly.

"No need!" Felicity said. "Florence said she'll finish them off with her brand new power. Look!"

Below them, Florence spun the bracelet on her wrist so that the blue gem on the side was on top instead of her usual red one. She breathed across the gem, and it turned her breath into a blast of ice. Ice flew everywhere, freezing the rest of the minions in huge swathes. The battle was over in seconds.

Kendra had to admit, she was impressed. "I didn't realize Pink Dragon's ice power would be so useful."

"Me, neither," Felicity said brightly. "All I got was a mild healing power and the ability to grow seeds."

"I know," Kendra said dryly. "Please attempt to power up again soon."

Felicity giggled, as if it had been a joke.

All the same, Felicity's power-up had been pretty good. Even a minor healing power was nice to have on a team, and her magic was more well-balanced now.

"You know," Kendra said out loud, "we all look more impressive now that we have full-sized wings growing out of our backs instead of little ones hovering behind us."

"The little ones were cute!" Felicity said.

"They were," Kendra said, "but these are better."

"I miss the little ones," Felicity said wistfully. "I keep hitting these big ones on minions when I turn around."

Kendra didn't. The little hovering wings had been so . . . so . . . *twelve-year-old*. Granted, Kendra had been twelve years old when she'd designed her magical girl form, and the other two girls had designed theirs to match hers. It wasn't that she'd disliked the little wings; she hadn't been dissatisfied with them at all. But the full-sized wings were just outright cool.

In fact, it was really a shame that they weren't doing anything to get exposure right now. They hadn't been on TV since defeating Dark Deathwave, Florence had refused to volunteer as a police aide anymore, and even the minions they were fighting were worthless ceramic without brains in their heads.

"I wish somebody could see us," Kendra complained.

"Why?" Felicity asked.

"Because we look so cool! We could win — win beauty contests like this!"

"Then why don't we enter some?" Felicity asked.

Kendra looked at her ditzy teammate in exasperation. "For one thing, pageants aren't designed for magical girls. For another, we are *so* much cooler than that."

"Then why don't we enter a competition for magical girls?" Florence asked.

Kendra spun around, startled. Florence had flapped her pink bat wings and risen in the air behind her. All three of them were now hovering above the frozen battlefield.

"Would you want to do that?" Kendra asked slowly.

"Sure. Why not?" Florence shrugged. "It sounds fun."

"Ooh!" Felicity squealed. "When we pose, I could make flowers bloom all around us!"

That . . . sounded pretty awesome, actually.

"Do you really want to do it?" Kendra asked cautiously. "There's a Magical Girl Team of the Year Competition in three months. We could register for it, if you really want to."

"Let's do it, then," Florence said.

Kendra stared at her best friend in amazement. *Who are you, and what did you do with the person who usually shoots down every interesting plan I have?*

"You're not the only one who's sick of fighting boring minions," Florence said, rolling her eyes. "Our new powers and new poses aren't worth much if we don't use them for something exciting. This sounds exciting, *and* not dangerous."

The fact that it wasn't dangerous was a downside to Kendra, but anything was better than the same repetitive battles every week. After all, they might attract a new arch-nemesis there. And even if they didn't, when they won, their reputations would be secure.

Of course, she wouldn't mention that she was hoping to attract a new arch-nemesis who might want to pick a fight with them after seeing them on TV. Kendra wasn't stupid. Mentioning that would no doubt snap Florence's enthusiasm shut right there.

"We have to practice poses!" Felicity cried, jumping up and down. "Let's do a brand new one! A brand new one with me in the middle!"

"*I'm* the one who should be in the middle," Florence shot back, "seeing as I'm the most powerful magical girl."

"You're both missing the point," Kendra said irritably. "I'm the team leader and the one who started this team. That makes me the main magical girl. Traditionally, the main magical girl gets top billing."

They both rounded on her.

"That's not fair!" Felicity cried.

"Who says you're the main magical girl?" Florence added.

"I'm the team leader! That means you're both my sidekicks! Haven't you ever watched TV?"

"TV is not reality!" Florence yelled.

"I'm not a sidekick!" Felicity complained.

Kendra snorted. *Really? The girl who can't fight alone in a battle thinks that?*

"Look," Florence said viciously, jabbing her finger in the air, "I powered up before anyone else, right? That makes me the main magical girl."

"And I got my powers before either of you!" Felicity cried. "That makes me the main magical girl!"

Kendra hesitated. Those were both true.

Florence had powered up immediately after turning her back on her evil boyfriend and reaffirming her choice to be a magical girl who did good. Her intense desire to be reborn as a better person had triggered the first power-up, before either Kendra or Felicity.

And as for magic . . . yes, *technically* Felicity had been a magical girl before either of them. She'd been a huge fan of the cartoon *Princess Prickly Pear,* and had created her own magical girl form in order to imitate her favorite character. That did not, in Kendra's opinion, count. But *technically* Felicity's original magical girl form had come before Cream Angel, Pink Dragon, or Green Fairy.

They both had a solid point. And if Kendra kept insisting that the central figure be her, they would likely gang up on her, and she'd wind up with Felicity in the middle of the team pose.

"Okay," Kendra said. "Florence, you can be in the center."

"Yesssssssssss!" Florence cried, pumping her arm in triumph.

"No fair," Felicity pouted.

"You were in the middle of our first pose in our first year, weren't you?" Kendra asked. "It's Florence's turn."

"Oh." Felicity seemed struck by that. "I guess so."

Kendra didn't add that that reason had nothing to do with it. She did value Felicity as a teammate, but the fact remained that Green Fairy was the weakest and least visually impressive of them. Yes, she looked solid as part of the team, but as a central figure, she'd be underwhelming. There was something about her that was unrelentingly a sidekick.

When you had an angel and a demon on the same team, one of them had to be in the center. Period. And if it couldn't be the angel, then it had to be the demon.

Yes, yes, Florence got super offended when you called her magical girl form that. But seriously. She had bat wings.

"Dragon wings!" Florence would snarl if you ever tried to point out the obvious.

All things considered, it was pretty funny that the girl on their team who was devoutly religious was the one who looked kind of villainish.

She'd picked fights over that before, because Florence's huffy attitude about her magical girl form was kind of hilarious, but she wasn't going to do that now. Not today. Today, the team was unified and had a goal that they all wanted to achieve.

Kendra held out her hand. "We're going to do this. And we're going to win."

Felicity put her hand in the center. "We're going to win!"

Florence thrust her hand in, too. "We're going to win!"

There was no doubt about it, Kendra reflected with satisfaction. They were the Wings of Justice.

They were going to win.

Chapter 2
The Friends

And the winner of the Magical Girl Team of the Year Award is . . ."

Girls all over the auditorium took deep breaths. Some jerked out of their poses, even though they weren't supposed to. The audience sitting in front of the stage had their attention fixed on the man with short hair wearing a business shirt and tie. All eyes in the immense hall were fixed on the announcer.

All eyes except Kendra's. She remained ramrod still, holding her pose. She had seen the announcer along with the other judges when they'd come by judging poses and powers, and breaking her focus now wouldn't change any results.

A flicker of nervousness coiled in her gut. At the very last minute, Florence had chickened out and made them use their earliest team pose, the one with Felicity in the center. Kendra had known it looked lame and protested, but there had been no time to argue, and yelling at each other wouldn't have made them look good, so she had been forced to acquiesce.

"Oh, please, please, please, please . . ." a girl in the team pose beside theirs was whispering.

Pray all you want, Kendra thought with irritation. *It's not going to change the results now.*

"... Victory's Bloom!" the man shouted.

Kendra jerked out of her pose. Her perfect self-control cracked. *What?*

"YES!" screamed the girl in the pose beside theirs, the one who had been whispering a few seconds earlier. She leapt down from their team pose on top of three boxes and flung her arms in the air, jumping up and down. "YES, YES, YES!"

Kendra couldn't feel anything. Her mind was too jammed with shock.

"Second place ..." the announcer said.

Is us, Kendra thought, swallowing.

"... is Seasonal Spices!"

Screaming came from the other side of the immense hall. Kendra's head whipped to the side, and she saw four girls in the distance hugging each other and jumping up and down.

How is this possible? Kendra thought numbly. *This can't ... this can't ... we're going to be third?*

"Third place ... is Twittering Sunshine!"

What? WHAT?! We're not even third?!?!

"Fourth place ... is Magenta Moonlight!"

By this point, Kendra was speechless with rage. *STUPID FLORENCE CHICKENING OUT!!*

"Fifth place ... is Puppy Darlings!"

Squeals and terribly fake woofing came from off to the right.

Kendra wanted to weep.

"Sixth place ... is Wings of Justice!"

"That's us!" Florence screamed. "That's us!"

"We won! We won! We won! We won!" Felicity screamed.

Kendra felt no joy. Only fury. How could they be so excited? Didn't they understand that they'd failed?

"Seventh place ..." the announcer continued.

WHO CARES?! Kendra wanted to scream.

He got all the way to tenth place, but she'd stopped listening. Her teammates, meanwhile, were babbling excitedly.

"Sixth place! Out of a hundred and eight teams!" Florence was saying excitedly. "That's really good!"

"It's almost like winning first place!" Felicity squealed.

It's WHAT?! Are you out of your mind?! Are you completely insane?! Kendra wanted to scream.

The announcer finished declaring tenth place, and the last excited squeals and babbling burst out across the auditorium. He waited a few seconds for the hubbub to settle down.

"Now, let us introduce our three special winners to you!" the announcer cried. "Victory's Bloom, come forward!"

The three girls of that team ran up to the stage. One was a girl with pigtails in a dark magenta cute-and-funky outfit, one had short dirty blonde hair and a green dress that was trying too hard to look cute, and the third had long blonde hair and wore an elegant grey and blue dress with a skirt that looked like tulip petals.

"Let's introduce them one at a time!" the announcer called, walking over to the girls as they reached the top of the stage. The girl in green was slightly pudgy and still panting for breath after running up the six stairs to get up to the stage. Naturally, he chose her first. "There's Geranium, the avatar of courage, with the magical power of sound!"

The girl panted and looked back and forth, seeming panicked. Noticing the audience focused on her, her cheeks glowed pink and she gave an awkward and jerky wave.

"Demonstrate your power for us," the announcer urged.

The girl's face flushed deeply, but she took a deep breath and sang into the man's microphone. The note was clear and in perfect pitch, and it shot a targeted shockwave across the room. Kendra felt it whoosh by her a split second before the platform that girl had been standing on for their team pose exploded.

"Wonderful!" the announcer praised. "Such a versatile power!"

Florence's power is far more versatile than that, Kendra thought snidely. *Did they even notice that she can breathe fire, ice, or poison?*

The announcer moved on to the next girl, the one in the elegant grey and blue dress. She was slender and expressionless. "There's Primrose, the avatar of hope, with the magical power of illusion!"

Without prompting, Primrose raised a baton and waved it around herself. Her costume changed color.

"Ooooh . . ." several people in the audience said.

Are you kidding me? Kendra thought incredulously. *Felicity's way more impressive than that. She can grow any plant instantly, as long as she has a seed!*

"And that brings us to the final member!" the announcer called, drawing out his words for effect. "Best of all . . ."

Excitedly, Geranium patted her hands in the air, creating a drumroll effect.

"The leader of the team . . ."

Expressionlessly, Primrose twirled her baton and created sparkles to surround their team leader.

"Mistletoe, the avatar of love, with the magical powers of clairvoyance, healing, singing, farseeing, telepathy, shapeshifting, teleportation, and of course her Valentine Finishing Blow!"

The audience gasped, and there was an excited babble across the room.

Kendra's mouth fell open. *How does one magical girl have that many powers?! Especially when her teammates only have one?!*

It would be one thing if all of those powers had been really lame, like "being able to make dishes wash themselves." But some of those powers were super rare and powerful. Shapeshifting? Telepathy? Teleportation?

They didn't even sound like they matched a unified theme, and that made no sense at all! Magical girls didn't just get random magic when they powered up; they either changed their magical girl form altogether, or they developed powers that enhanced whatever theme they'd already been using.

Maybe she had some sort of luck-based power originally, Kendra thought, her mind racing. *She could have a number of really powerful magical abilities at her call, but it depends on luck which one is available . . .*

There'd been a magical girl like that back in the sixties. Kendra's mom had written a biography about her a few years ago. She'd gone by the ridiculously long name Child of Flowers and Dice.

But no.

"That's an amazing assortment!" the announcer said into his microphone. "I'm sure we're all curious about your original power!"

"Clairvoyance!" Mistletoe said happily.

Clairvoyance? Kendra thought incredulously. *How the heck?!*

Farseeing, telepathy . . . okay, both of those made sense as a logical extension of Mistletoe's first power. She could see where those had come from.

Healing, maybe. That was a common power for fighting magical girls in teams.

But a finishing blow, too? That was weird. You might see both together in a solo magical girl, but when a girl was part of a team, you expected to see healing and the most powerful finishing blow held by different people.

And where in the world had singing, shapeshifting, and teleportation come into it?

"Amazing!" the man said. "How strong are those powers?"

Mistletoe giggled. "Pretty powerful, I guess. Do you want to see all of them?"

"Yes!" the audience shouted.

"We can't hear you!" the announcer called into his microphone.

"YES!!" the audience roared.

Mistletoe grinned and waved her hand. A heart-shaped ring with diamonds and ribbons affixed appeared in it. Even from this far away, Kendra could tell her focus item had developed frills of justice several times.

"Love's Miraculous Teleport!" Mistletoe called, holding the heart-shaped ring over her head. A shower of pink hearts appeared out of nowhere, scattered around her, and she vanished. Then she appeared in the same place.

The audience screamed and applauded.

Probably short-range and very flashy, Kendra noted. *Useless for stealth.*

"Love's Beautiful Song!"

Light shaped like a heart glowed at Mistletoe's throat, and she sang a verse of a hit pop song.

The audience cheered again.

Completely useless, Kendra thought. *That's just autotune magic. Almost every singing magical girl has it, and having to have a glowing light at your throat while you use it looks dumb.*

"Love's Healing Wind!" Mistletoe cried, pointing at the platform near Kendra that Geranium's soundwave had destroyed.

The platform immediately glowed and reassembled itself.

Kendra's eyebrows raised. *Okay, that was impressive. Not all healing powers can fix inanimate objects.*

"Love's Mind Ray!" Mistletoe put the heart-shaped ring to her forehead and scanned the audience with squinted eyes. "That boy! He has a crush on me!"

A boy in the audience blushed furiously and hid under his seat. The audience laughed.

So it's telepathy that can only be used to find out whether a boy likes her, Kendra noted. *That definitely fits with her original power and theme.*

"Love's Alternate Costumes!" Mistletoe switched between four different variations of her magical girl outfit.

The audience applauded and whistled.

That's supposed to be a shapeshifting power? Unlike the overly enthusiastic audience, Kendra was profoundly unimpressed. *I mean, technically a magical girl's costume is part of her body, so being able to switch outfits while transformed is a form of shapeshifting, but it's the weakest kind imaginable.*

"Love's Farseeing Ray!" Once again, Mistletoe put her focus item to her forehead. "And the furthest away boy who has a crush on me is . . . one of Queen Hemlock's minions!"

The audience burst into titters.

Once again, the love theme and the limitation, Kendra noted. *Hang on, wait! Queen Hemlock is attacking them, too? That's so rude! How many other magical girl teams is our arch-nemesis cheating on us with?!*

And by the sound of things, Queen Hemlock had been sending Victory's Bloom *actual* minions, not the ceramic variety controlled by the Princess of Poison. Kendra was very offended.

It was one thing winning the contest we were supposed to win, but now they're fighting with our arch-villain, too? Ugh!

For the first time, Kendra wondered just how many teams their arch-nemesis was fighting. Was it possible she only used the ceramic minions for the magical girls she didn't take seriously? That would explain why nothing interesting ever happened in their battles.

Kendra's blood boiled. It was true, the Wings of Justice hadn't been taking those fights seriously. Those ceramic minions were nothing but a repetitive grind. But if they needed to take those battles seriously to get their enemy's attention, they would. Nobody was going to kill Queen Hemlock before they did.

Kendra completely ignored the rest of Mistletoe's powers as she started working on battle plans. There were a lot of things they could be doing better. As soon as they got home, she and her teammates would start training.

Missy was having the time of her life. Her teammates never wanted to see her show off her powers. Gerry was always polite and just said she'd seen them all before, but Rose could be downright rude. It was a shame she was almost done. She would've loved to stand here all day.

"Love's Sleepy Clairvoyance!" Missy proclaimed, touching her heart to her forehead.

The audience leaned forward.

"I have to fall asleep before it'll work," she added sheepishly.

The audience burst into laughter.

"And finally . . ." Missy said.

Gerry obligingly started a drumroll behind her.

Missy spun around, tossed her heart in the air, caught it, made a complicated overhand and underhand pass, thew it up in the air again, and caught it in a crouched position. "Valentine Finishing Blow!"

An explosion of magenta light blasted out and bathed the auditorium in a warm fuzzy feeling.

Someone in the audience screamed and burst into flames. The rest of the audience yelped and screamed out of their seats.

"It's okay!" Missy called. "It only works on evil! That means he was an undercover minion here to spy on the winning teams!"

One of the audience members tentatively prodded the man who had screamed. The dead minion's skin was charred, but his clothes were untouched.

"He's wearing a villain costume under his coat!" the audience member reported. "I see spikes!"

Everyone relaxed, and went back to happy chattering.

Missy turned around and gave her teammates a brilliant smile. "I saved us all, and didn't even know it!" she mouthed.

Gerry applauded quietly. Rose just shrugged.

"That's an amazing power!" the announcer said into his microphone. "And what a privilege that we were able to see it in action today!"

The audience whistled and applauded with almost deafening volume. Missy basked in the attention.

"Why don't you tell us about how you got your powers?" the man asked, holding his microphone out in front of her.

Missy giggled. She still couldn't believe that she had made it, that she was standing here and being interviewed. It was such a dream come true! Literally, since she had dreamed about this. "Oh . . . well . . ."

She could remember it all like it was yesterday. That had been the most important days of her life. That had been the day she had become Mistletoe.

"It all began one night when I had a dream about becoming a legendary warrior," she said. "When I woke up, I had the talisman I'd dreamed about in my hands. What's more, the dream I had the next night showed me I needed to choose two teammates. Of course I gave one of *those* talismans to my best friend!"

She waved back at Gerry, who flushed pink and gave a tiny wave in response.

"That's quite an unusual beginning," the announcer said. "You dreamed about having magic before you got it?"

"Yeah," Missy said.

"But how is that possible?" he asked. "Most magical girls don't get their focus items until after they've decided to be magical girls. In fact, I can't think of a single one who's gotten a focus item first."

"Oh . . . well . . ." Missy giggled, embarrassed. "I think I might've been a magical girl before and just forgotten about it. My mom says when I was five, I used to run around with a toy I said was my focus item. She never saw me transform, so she figured I was just playing pretend. I guess I wasn't, though."

"Perhaps that would explain why you have so many more powers than your teammates!" the man said. "If you've had ten more years to develop them."

"Oh, no, no!" Missy giggled. "I only started with clairvoyance. I've gotten all the rest through power-ups in the past three years."

"But . . ." the announcer said, faltering. "How many power-ups have you had?"

"Only four," Missy said, waving her hand. "The first one got me farseeing. The second one got me singing and shapeshifting and my Valentine Finishing Blow. The third one got me telepathy. The fourth one got me healing and teleportation. My focus item didn't even change how it looked with the last power-up!"

The announcer swallowed. He looked over at the other judges, who were standing offstage. The other judges were murmuring.

Is something wrong? Missy thought, worried.

The announcer quickly recovered and handed her the microphone. "So tell us more about the start of your team!"

Missy giggled, taking it. "Oh, well, like I said, the other two talismans appeared in my hands when I woke up after the second dream. I gave one to Geranium because she was my best friend. Then we discovered that the new transfer student in our class had tremendous magical potential, which meant we had to make her our third teammate. She was overjoyed by the news!"

The judges' flurried discussion had resulted in one of the judges running up to the stage. She was a woman with her hair pulled back in a severe bun.

She took the microphone from the announcer.

"Let me clarify something," the woman said. "You say *their* focus items appeared to *you?*"

"Yeah," Missy said. "Because we were meant to be a team."

"*Their* focus items appeared to *you?*"

Why did she keep repeating that?

"Like, that's normal, isn't it?" Missy asked. "I mean, I'm the team leader."

The woman looked speechless.

"Is that *not* normal?" Rose asked sharply from behind them.

The woman judge shook herself. "No, it's . . . not normal. There's really only way that could happen, and it's very unusual. If you're not aware of what's going on, you ought to be."

Missy stared at the woman in alarm. Why did the judge look so serious?

The announcer leaned forward and whispered, "Is this the time or place?"

The judge waved him off with a sharp gesture and said into the microphone, looking at Missy's two teammates, "Mistletoe has a segmented focus item. That means it comes in multiple pieces. That's unusual except with things like earrings that are naturally in pairs, but it's not unheard of. What's *very* unusual is what you three have done."

Gerry looked baffled. "What did we do?"

"You took segments of her focus item," the judge said, "and made them *your* focus items. That means your magic is permanently linked to hers. All of your power-ups go to her. All of your costume changes go to her. That might explain why two of the costumes she shapeshifted between looked like frills of justice versions of yours."

Rose's face had gone completely blank.

"That's not true!" Missy burst out. "I've never taken anything that belongs to them! I've just powered up more because I'm the main magical girl!"

"You've powered up more," the judge said sharply, "because you're the only one of the three who *ever will.* And if the other two aren't aware of that, they really need to be!"

The announcer finally wrestled the microphone away from her.

"Ha ha!" he said uncomfortably, looking rather desperate. "Well, that's our Magical Girl Team of the Year! Who knew that they were so closely connected, eh? What a special and unique situation, choosing to share powers that way! Now, let's move on to the closing ceremonies —"

"No!" Missy burst out. "You're trying to make us sound horrible! That's not how it is at all! Things were right from the moment we first battled together. We're an invincible team; no villain has ever been able to stand against our triple teamwork. We're *friends!*"

"So how *do* you three work together?" the announcer asked, holding the microphone out to her. "How have you been winning your most recent battles?"

"Well . . ." Missy said. "Recently, Geranium's been scouting ahead to figure out the terrain. Primrose distracts any of Queen Hemlock's minions that lie waiting for us. And then, when they least expect it, we join forces and defeat them!"

Two voices murmured behind her.

"Join . . ."

". . . forces?"

"Sounds like a successful battle strategy!" the man said.

"Oh, yes!" Missy agreed, relaxing. They were back to talking about how wonderful her team was. "Of course, our current archenemy, Queen Hemlock, is particularly nasty, so our teamwork has to be impeccable —"

"*Impeccable?!*" an outraged voice shouted from behind her.

Startled, Missy turned to face her teammate who had spoken. Why did Rose look mad?

"Primrose?" Missy asked hesitantly. "What's wrong?"

Rose looked like she was about to explode. "What do you think? I'm not your teammate — I'm your *sidekick!* Everything we do is all about *you!*"

"Oooooooooooooooooooooooooooooooooooooooooh . . ." the audience murmured, chatter rolling across the people in the seats.

"About *me?*" Missy asked, rather panicked. She put her hand to her chest. "But we do everything together!"

"Together?" Rose sneered. "Yes. But when have we three ever been equals?"

The announcer stirred, looking concerned. He raised his microphone to speak, but Rose kept talking and cut him off.

"Your transformation scene is three times longer than ours."

"Geranium's has more sparkles —"

"You get *all* the power-ups."

"But that's just because I always defeat —!"

"No, it's *not!* We just *learned* that it's not! Singing and healing were clearly meant to be Geranium's powers, and shapeshifting and teleportation were clearly supposed to be mine!"

"It appears this team wasn't aware just how closely tied they were," the announcer said with a nervous laugh and a look at the audience. "So, let's talk more about your beginning! Who was the first archenemy you three fough—"

But Rose just talked more loudly. "And *every single boy we meet* seems to fall in love with you, *including* half the villains!"

Missy rubbed her head sheepishly. She'd noticed that fact. She suspected it was a passive power she'd gotten at some point. "Eheheh . . ."

"About your first enemy —" the announcer tried desperately.

"Did it ever occur to you that we might want to help save the world, too?" Rose demanded. "That that might be the *reason* we joined your team?"

Gerry raised a hand hesitantly up near her face. "Umm, I just joined because Mistletoe was my friend . . ."

"We distract villains," Rose snapped. "You save the day. What part of that is *teamwork?*"

"B-but you've saved us from things before!" Missy protested. "Alone! Like that evil alarm clock last year!"

"Yeah, when you had a fever of a hundred and two and couldn't get out of bed," Rose snorted. "Big deal."

Missy was starting to feel panicked. This was supposed to be a glorious victory. Why was everything falling apart?

"We're a team!" she said desperately. "We're best friends in the whole wide world! We're —"

"We're throwaway minions to you, just like the ones Queen Hemlock uses!" Rose shouted.

"But Primrose, that's not fair!" Gerry burst out. "She's the one who *gave* us our powers! And, anyway —"

Missy burst into tears and ran off the stage.

"Ummm . . ." the announcer said slowly into the microphone. "I suggest we take a ten minute break . . ."

Chapter 3
The Break

Huddled backstage with a bunch of boxes and a silent teammate who had just had a complete meltdown, Gerry was at a loss for words.

"Rose?" she said tentatively.

Rose said nothing. She just sat in silence, still transformed as Primrose, with her bangs over her face.

The silence stretched on, and on, and on. For all that Gerry was timid, she couldn't take it any longer.

"*Why?*" she burst out finally, clutching her wand to her chest. "Why did you say that in front of a live audience?"

Rose didn't move.

"Surely you didn't really mean it! And now Security has to search to find Mistletoe!"

Rose moved slightly. Her head was still ducked so the bangs covered her face. "I'm sorry, Geranium. I didn't mean to blurt everything out in public like that. But I *did* mean what I said."

Gerry swallowed, and swallowed again. If Rose was that unhappy . . . if Rose was that unhappy, then . . .

Wait! A solution occurred to her!

"Well, I guess if you really feel like that, Mistletoe and I could find some way to make sure you get the next power-up," Gerry said with relief. "Now that we know what's going on, we should be able to shift the next one over you or me. I don't mind not getting any, so you can get all the rest from now on . . ."

"That's nice of you, Geranium, but no," Rose cut her off. Her head was still ducked, the bangs still covering her face. "I'm sick of everything. I'm leaving."

"You . . ." A spike of panic shot through Gerry. "You just mean, like, the competition . . . right?"

Rose was silent for a long moment. "Wrong."

She stood up slowly and picked up her focus item, the grey and blue baton with purple sheer tulle draping from it. She held the baton above her head, and a circle of sparkles engulfed her, swishing down from her raised arm to her toes.

She was now only Rose, standing there in a pair of jeans and a blue T-shirt.

"Prim—" Gerry began.

Rose's silence was eloquent. So much that it shut Gerry up.

Gerry tried to summon up the courage to say something. Anything. Something that would fix this. Anything that would stop her friend from leaving.

Rose set the baton on a box and walked towards the exit. "That's the last time you'll ever see me transform."

"*PRIMROSE!*" Gerry cried, finally capable of speaking again.

But Rose was already out the door.

SLAM!

Geranium sat there, frozen, her arms outstretched from where she had been reaching out for her lost teammate. Slowly, she pulled them back in. She fell to the ground in blackest despair.

Memories engulfed her. Memories of everything she'd had and now lost.

Missy holding out the two cute talismans to her after school. *"Pick one!"*

Gerry had been so flattered, so excited, so pleased to be chosen despite being pudgy and shy and nobody's idea of an ideal teammate.

She remembered Missy chasing down the new girl at school. *"I'm sure you have tremendous magical potential! I'm very, very, very sure! I saw it in a dream! You have to be our teammate!"*

The Break

She remembered the look of horror on Rose's face, which had been so hilarious at the time because Missy had completely missed it.

She remembered Missy's silly theory about their powers. *"Do you think our powers come from things we're* weak *in? I mean, courage for Geranium, who's so shy, hope for Primrose, who's sort of cynical . . ."* Then a long pause that became increasingly sheepish. *"Er . . . love . . . which I hope I'm not weak in . . ."*

Missy's excited face a few weeks ago. *"Guess what? I've entered our team in the biggest magical girl competition!"*

Their team pose less than an hour ago, which they had done a thousand times before. *"We're Victory's Bloom!"*

And now it would be the last time they ever did.

Gerry started to sob, mourning over her lost team, her lost friendship, her lost dreams. Everything was gone now. Everything was ruined. Why had they become friends, only to have it end this way?

"Victory's . . . Bloom . . ." she sobbed, lost in grief.

"Look! It's Geranium!" an unfamiliar voice shouted.

Gerry looked up, startled. She saw a pigtailed child standing at the entrance to the backstage. "Wh— What?"

"Can I get your autograph?!" the little girl squealed. "You guys are, like, my favorite team ever! You're always fighting bad guys in my town, so I bet you live where I do! I was hoping you would win the whole time!"

Gerry fumbled, lost in social situations to begin with, but especially too shattered to deal with this one. "B-but . . . our team just . . ."

"I brought you a piece of paper!" the little girl cried, yanking a crumpled piece of paper out of her pocket. She held it out. "Sign it for me! Say, 'To Chelsea!'"

"CHELSEA!" another voice yelled from behind them. "What did I tell you about running backstage?!"

Gerry's head whipped over, and she saw a woman with two buns at the back of her neck glaring at the small child. Gerry looked back at the child, who stuck her tongue out at the woman, and then she looked back at the woman. The child's mother?

The woman leaned against the doorway in exhaustion. "I'm so sorry . . . I don't know what possessed her to run back here like this. Especially given what you're probably going through . . ."

She glanced down at the baton sitting on the box. Gerry had the feeling the mother understood what had just happened, even though the daughter didn't.

She glanced down at the baton sitting on the box. Gerry had the feeling the mother understood what had just happened, even though the daughter didn't.

"Autograph! Autograph!" the little girl shouted. "And then I'll give you *my* autograph! So when I'm a Victory's Bloom, it'll be worth a fortune!"

The woman got a pained look on her face. As if to explain the child's audacity, she said, "My daughter idolizes you . . . She keeps saying she wants to be one of you when she grows up . . ."

"Autograph, autograph, autograph!" the little girl squealed, holding out the paper and jumping up and down.

A strange idea rose in Gerry's mind. It was a ridiculous idea. A crazy idea. And yet . . .

Missy wanted teammates, didn't she? Two teammates, in fact. If she hadn't wanted teammates extremely badly, her focus item wouldn't have segmented itself into three. True, the consequences hadn't been what Missy had intended, but Gerry didn't mind it. Maybe . . . maybe if they had another teammate, one who wouldn't mind using a segment, that would be enough for Missy.

Slowly, Gerry looked up.

"One . . . of us?" she murmured.

Gerry wanted Rose back. She wanted Primrose so badly that she could barely contain the ache. But Primrose was gone. She wasn't coming back. And Victory's Bloom couldn't be Victory's Bloom without a third teammate.

Mistletoe couldn't be Mistletoe without a third teammate.

I'm not useless, Gerry realized with amazement. *My being a magical girl is what makes Mistletoe so powerful. She wouldn't power up nearly as much without me. I'm not just a silly scout to check the terrain — I'm essential!*

It was a wonderful realization. And that hardened her resolution.

Gerry got up and seized the baton from the box. It was as intact as ever, despite the fact that Rose had abandoned it. Of course it was. It couldn't have crumbled. It wasn't just Primrose's focus item — it was Mistletoe's, too.

And now it would belong to somebody else.

"Know why we're strong?" Missy had proudly told the two of them once. *"Because we weren't one of those teams that a bunch of mascots picked out. We three* chose *each other!"*

"I'm sick of everything." Rose had been so sure, so certain. She hadn't even looked back. *"I'm leaving."*

The woman was still talking. Perhaps she had been talking all this time, and Gerry just hadn't been listening. "She even has pajamas that she puff-painted your team symbol on —"

"Mommm!" the little girl protested. "You weren't supposed to *tell* her that!"

Gerry took a deep breath. She had to figure out a way to ask. It wasn't too much to ask this girl, surely?

"I'm sorry . . ." the woman said quickly, noticing her deep breath. "I'll get my daughter out of your hair . . ."

"No. Wait," Gerry said softly, summoning her courage. "Let me find Mistletoe. I have something I want to ask her."

Rumors had been flying and buzzing around the auditorium, between the members of the audience and the girls of the one hundred and seven losing teams.

Everyone had opinions.

Everyone thought they understood the implications.

Everyone was an idiot.

For all that Kendra loved flashy magic, she was a little too practical-minded to want it herself. Having to shout the names of attacks before using them seemed silly. Instead, while transformed, she had slightly better reflexes, strength, speed, and senses than usual. This, of course, included hearing.

Standing casually by a pillar just outside the range at which anyone would realize she was capable of it, Kendra eavesdropped on the judges' conversation.

"Should we rescind the title?" one of the judges was saying.

"We can't do that," the announcer said.

"Why not? We have rules about cheating," a woman challenged. She was the judge who had gone up on the stage to tell everyone about Mistletoe's segmented focus item.

"They weren't technically cheating," the announcer argued. "There was nothing in the rules about this situation."

"But it's an embarrassment," a male judge complained. "That one girl, Primrose, is probably going to quit. Can you imagine the headlines tomorrow? 'Magical Girl Team of the Year Dissolves On Stage!'"

"And whose fault would that be?" the announcer muttered, eyeing the woman judge with dislike.

"I refuse to apologize for telling those two girls exactly what they needed to know."

"You could have waited until *after* the competition!"

"Why would I do that? It was good for the audience to hear. We don't want more teams seeking to emulate Victory's Bloom's gross power imbalance next year."

"You voted for them! Knowing their 'gross power imbalance'!" a male judge cried.

"I assumed that two of them were high-powered specialists and one was a low-powered generalist," the woman said coldly. "It was the natural assumption to make. That's an unusual team composition, so it made them the most interesting team here. Besides, I might add, it turned out that they *were* the most interesting team here, just for all the wrong reasons."

"If we rescind the title, we could give it to someone who really deserves it," the male judge argued.

Kendra's heart pounded, and her wings lifted a fraction. *Like Wings of Justice!*

"Like Seasonal Spices," he added.

Kendra's heart dropped like a stone. *Oh, right. We weren't second.*

"I'm sure the Seasonal Spices girls are lovely," the announcer said, "but have you thought about what that would mean? There are ten minutes left in the show. We wouldn't have time to interview anybody. And if they won, they'd be ineligible to win it next year, which they have a real chance of doing. Why would you deny them the chance to win the spotlight for real, rather than being an afterthought?"

Kendra hated him for not thinking the Wings of Justice had a real shot at winning next year.

"Look, whatever we do," a second woman judge said, "there's no damage control we can do here. We can't just play this off as a publicity stunt if their team fractures. Let's just wrap this show up and get it over with."

And give the title to Wings of Justice first, Kendra thought, rustling her wings impatiently. *That would be good.*

A woman with two buns at the back of her neck rushed over. She started talking to the judges in rapid whispers. Kendra strained, but unfortunately couldn't hear a word of it because she was standing a little too far away.

The judges reacted with surprise. The female judge was incredulous. The announcer's eyebrows raised.

"Well, that would be a solution," he said, just loud enough that Kendra could hear.

What? Kendra thought. *WHAT?!*

Ten minutes later, when the program was scheduled to end, people were getting out of their seats and picking up programs and starting to murmur as they headed toward the doors. The announcer ran up on the stage and waved his hands frantically.

"Welcome back, guests!" he called loudly into his microphone. "We have an unexpected development! We hadn't realized this, but the team had been planning to disband, anyway. And it seems that Victory's Bloom has chosen this moment . . . to unveil their brand-new teammate, Peony!"

Kendra's jaw dropped. *Say what?!*

A little girl came prancing onto the stage. She had her hair in pigtails with ribbons around them, and wore an outfit that was . . . sort of similar to Primrose's, except that it looked silly and had tomboyish shorts instead of an elegant tulip-like skirt.

"I AM PEONY!" the girl exclaimed. She spun around and tried to flip the baton up in the air, which fell to the ground and clattered. Undaunted, she grabbed it. "I'm a Victory's Bloom! I'm amazing!"

"Um," the announcer said, "I think you mean you're a member of Victory's Bloom . . ."

"I'm one of the Victory's Blooms!"

"A team name's not used that wa— never mind. Mistletoe, Geranium, come tell us what you think of your new teammate!"

Very appalled? Kendra thought, her nose wrinkling.

Mistletoe moved forward gingerly. She had a rather shellshocked and uncertain look on her face. Kendra couldn't blame her. She took the microphone that was offered and said, "W-well, Primrose was planning to leave after the competition, and we'd already chosen Peony to replace her, so, like, this was planned all along . . ."

Really? Kendra thought incredulously. *You're really trying to play it that way? Who's going to fall for that?*

Felicity grabbed Kendra's arm. "I'm so glad they already had another teammate!" she whispered excitedly.

Kendra gave Felicity a flat stare.

She looked over at Florence, who rolled her eyes as if to say, *I'm not responsible for our teammate's ditziness.*

Kendra let out a small snort of laughter. To her surprise, she realized she was glad they hadn't won the competition. Better the humiliation of sixth place than to wind up like Victory's Bloom, fragmented and trying to make a completely ridiculous excuse.

Wings of Justice was awesome. The three of them knew it, and that was all that mattered.

It didn't matter if the judges didn't know it. It didn't matter if the audience didn't know it. It didn't matter if Queen Hemlock didn't know it . . . okay, yes it did, and Kendra was *totally* going to start pushing her friends to show that blasted villain that it wasn't okay to underestimate her team. Because, seriously!

But other than that, things were okay. They were a strong and capable and well-balanced team.

Pink Dragon, with her fire, ice, and poison breath.

Green Fairy, with her plant-growing and minor healing power.

Cream Angel, with her boomerang halo and unusually strong senses and speed.

They'd be friends forever. They'd be magical girls until they outgrew their powers. And unlike Victory's Bloom, nobody would ever break up their team.

Chapter 4
The Fix

Someone pushed a button on the remote, and the broadcast of the Magical Girl Team of the Year competition winked out and died.

"I love it," a woman declared. She was dressed in a miniskirt and cape, with low-cut cleavage showing. There were spikes all over her costume, and an upside-down crown on her head. She held a scepter in her hand, which she also held upside-down. "It was past time, but I love it."

Beside her was a silent girl with long blonde hair. Bangs covered her face.

"And when I say that it was past time, I mean it was *really* past time," the woman continued relentlessly. "How many months has it been now, Nightshade?"

The girl said nothing.

"Say something!" the woman snapped. "For crying out loud!"

"Well, Mom, I quit," the girl said dully, not looking up. "I broke our championship team. Just like you wanted."

"Yes, only five months after I ordered you to," Queen Hemlock snorted. "Honestly, Nightshade, I was beginning to wonder where your loyalties lay."

"We were teammates for *three years*, Mom!" the girl exploded. "And on your orders, no less! They thought we were friends."

"Which *will* work to our advantage in demoralizing them, true," Queen Hemlock said, drumming her fingers along the edge of her upside-down scepter. "And breaking your team in front of that live audience *was* a master stroke. But we're still behind in our plans. So, when you go back to reveal yourself as Queen Hemlock's daughter —"

"Wait . . ." Nightshade said slowly. "You expect me to go *back* to my old teammates as a villain?"

"Don't be stupid, Nightshade," her mother said, folding her arms. "Why, exactly, did you think I ordered you to join when their leader recruited you?"

"As an infiltrator," Nightshade said.

Nobody would ever expect a minion to be capable of being a magical girl. You had to be both young and innocent, and minions were usually adults and anything but. But Nightshade had been a special case. Nightshade had been only three months old.

Nightshade was a humunculus. A special kind that had taken a lot of her mother's magic to create. One with a will of its own.

"As an infiltrator," her mother confirmed. "And what do infiltrators do?"

"Get information."

"In order to . . .?"

"I don't know." She'd tried not to think about it. She'd tried never to think about being a villain whenever she'd been with her friends. She liked them better.

Or rather, she *had* liked them better before she'd learned that Mistletoe had been using her. Now she just felt broken inside.

Queen Hemlock snorted. "Your infiltration will have taught you all their weak points — *and* the weak points of solo magical girls and magical girl teams in general, too. You know that. You've crushed hundreds by now. You're going to defeat Victory's Bloom next, and it's going to be easy."

"Defeat them," Nightshade said numbly. "You expect me to face my former teammates and . . . defeat them."

It was bad enough to have to face them. She had planned to never return to their school.

But defeat them? Break their focus items, or slaughter their magical girl forms? How could she do that? How could anyone?

She'd expected her mom to understand. She'd known her mom would pulverize the team eventually once she left it, which was why she had resisted quitting, but she'd expected that her mother would send different minions. Hired minions. Maybe disposable minions. Not Nightshade. Not her strongest one. Not her best.

Didn't she understand that everyone had limits?

"Not just *them!*" Queen Hemlock said gleefully. "Destroying Victory's Bloom will be only the *beginning!* That competition gave us some fantastic leads on where to focus on next. Once we've eliminated every major team finalist, the path will be clear for us to *easily —*"

Her tirade was interrupted by a loud *Beeeep!*

"Oh, that's another of my hired minions coming back from defeat. Excuse me while I go chew him out."

The door slammed on her way out.

Nightshade sat there silently.

If Queen Hemlock was going to seriously attack Victory's Bloom, they wouldn't stand a chance. Of that, she was completely certain.

Mistletoe had no concept of battle strategies. She threw around flashy magic as if that alone was enough, and half the time didn't even hit the minions she was aiming at. Geranium was the worst scout ever. She never noticed any minions before they snuck up behind her to attack. Primrose had been using illusion to hide their incompetence from both of her teammates, and her mother, for years.

If her teammates had known they were incompetent, they wouldn't have thought they deserved power-ups, and so wouldn't have gotten them. She'd figured power-ups were their only chance to become strong enough to survive.

If their team's many enemies had realized that two of them were incompetent, they would have sent their best fighters at Primrose every time, thereby nullifying the effectiveness of her power, which was focused on stealth. Worse, if she'd been forced to fight openly, it might have caused her teammates to question why she was so much better at fighting than them.

But most importantly of all, if Queen Hemlock had noticed they were incompetent, she would have canceled the experiment and pulled Nightshade back right away. Which was the one thing that Nightshade, a.k.a. Primrose the magical girl, a.k.a. Rose the normal girl with friends, could not have allowed to happen.

But now the point was entirely moot. Because it turned out their friendship had been as much of a sham as her mother had wanted it to be all along.

Why don't I just let her do it? Nightshade thought bitterly. *Why don't I just let Mom squash them? Mistletoe deserves it. And even Geranium didn't balk at replacing me right away.*

But the thought of doing it herself . . .

She wanted to forget the whole thing and pretend Primrose had never existed. She wanted to bury herself in Nightshade, the minion who never showed any emotion, who never felt anything, who just did her job because it had to be done.

Because it had to be done . . .

How many magical girls have I destroyed because I made sure I never felt anything?

Nightshade looked up at the wall above the TV. There was a banner high above that said "Defeated Magical Girl Trophies." Underneath were focus items. Dozens of focus items. All of them from magical girls she'd killed.

Most focus items crumbled when a magical girl quit or had her magical girl form killed, because they owed their entire existence to magic. But those that had been physical objects beforehand survived to become the magicless objects they had been before. Those were the ones Nightshade had scooped up and taken home as trophies. She hardly knew why.

Her mother had loved the habit, gleefully creating her a wall to hang them on. She had shown the wall off to her villain friends many times, proudly proclaiming that it was a magnificent way to gloat and rub those former magical girls' faces in the fact that their magic had been destroyed. Those human girls who could no longer transform would not even have a memento remaining.

But that wasn't why Nightshade had taken them.

Perhaps I thought, she realized slowly, *that they might give me a way to escape.*

Nightshade had been able to become a magical girl because she was innocent. And innocent she had been. She hadn't recognized the difference between friendship and malice. Between kindness and cruelty. Between loyalty and slavery.

Mistletoe: *"I love you both sooooo much!"*

Queen Hemlock: *"Stop complaining and obey me!"*

Neither of them had truly deserved her loyalty. But one came a lot closer than the other:

The one who hadn't *purposefully* made her in order to use her.

Nightshade rocketed up to her feet and seized two of the trophies: a sword and a dagger that had probably belonged to intelligent magical girls who hadn't thought a hairbow or a genie lamp would be much better choices of weapons.

She'd become a magical girl because she was innocent. And she was no longer innocent. But there was something else that worked just as well to become a magical girl.

She could be *good.*

She had quit being a magical girl. By all accounts, that should be the end of it. But sometimes the magic system would allow a girl who was young enough and innocent enough, or good enough, to become one a second time. She had seen it before with girls whose magical girl forms she'd killed.

The magic system had been patient with her before. It had even let Nightshade transform invisibly on the battlefield and use Primrose's illusion powers for villain work.

Surely it would give her a second chance. Surely it would let her become a magical girl again if she intended to use magic for the right thing this time.

Please. Please. Please. Please . . .

Queen Hemlock stomped down the corridor, irate.

"And no more excuses, slackers!" she yelled over her shoulder. "Next time, you'll all go *together* to defeat the Wings of Justice!"

The Fix

What was she hiring minions for if they were just as useless as the ceramic ones? She'd sent one of the hired ones to fight that particular throwaway team right after the competition because Nightshade had been busy. What did he mean, "They're much more vicious than they used to be?" Imbecile! Magical girl teams didn't suddenly get better for no reason!

Maybe I ought to make some more like Nightshade, Queen Hemlock thought, storming down the hallway. *She's much more useful than those idiots. Saving up magic for another three years without using any would be a drag, but . . .*

She stormed through the doorway to the room where she had left Nightshade.

"Right, then," she said, picking up where they had left off. "I'm going to send you back in three weeks. Just enough time for them to have gotten used to the idea that they will never see you again, and not nearly enough time for them to have practiced much with their new teammate —"

She stopped abruptly. Nightshade was not where she'd left her. The girl was now standing near the doorway with a sword in one hand and a dagger in the other. And of all things, she was wearing a dark blue costume with a pleated skirt and stars all over it.

"Nightshade, what are you doing?" she asked impatiently. "That's a terrible costume. It looks like something a magical girl would wear. If you want something new, we can go to Rhea Korstanos Designs. We'd have to pull a heist or two to pay for it, though."

Nightshade said nothing.

Said nothing.

Said nothing.

"I'm betraying you," she said finally, with exasperation.

"*WHAT?*" Queen Hemlock shouted, snatching the scepter from her side and flipping it upside-down. "You can't do that!"

Paralysis mist burst from the scepter, but Nightshade was already moving. She dashed forward, avoiding the paralysis mist, lifted her mother up, and slammed the dagger into the wall. When she darted away, Queen Hemlock was dangling by the top of her cape that was pinned to the wall.

"Don't try to follow me, and no one gets hurt."

"You can't double-cross your mother!" Queen Hemlock screamed, squeezing her hands into fists. "I created you!"

"Yes, and now I've outgrown you," Nightshade said coldly. "*You're* the one who taught me how to double-cross!"

Blast! She'd forgotten this was one of the risks of creating intelligent humunculi. She'd been warned that things like this could happen, but Nightshade had always been so loyal that there'd seemed no need for worry.

Well, it was fine. She'd equipped the minion with a kill switch for this very reason. Queen Hemlock flipped her scepter right-side-up, spun the gemstone at the top upside-down, and a button appeared. She slammed her finger into it.

Nightshade stood with her arms folded, completely unaffected. "You know, the thing about a kill switch is that it's only useful if the target's not transformed into a magical form that doesn't have to have anything in common with the original body."

With a sinking feeling, Queen Hemlock realized she'd made a slight miscalculation. So *this* was why intelligent humunculi weren't used more often to become magical girls. Still —

She slashed the sharp edge of the gemstone across her cape, which sliced, ripped, and set her free.

She flipped her scepter to the side and aimed it. Forget paralysis or kill switches. She had more than a month's saved magic in the storage section, which meant she had more than enough to coat the entire room with corrosive acid. She spun the scepter, and the gemstone glowed —

She was knocked off balance by a whirlwind of bladed stars. *CRASH!*

She watched in horror as Nightshade slammed the scepter into the floor, shattering it.

"My scepter!" Queen Hemlock screamed.

"Magical girls aren't the only ones who lose their powers without their talismans, are they, Mom?" Nightshade asked with a chilly smile. "Now you only have access to the magic you generate second-by-second, which isn't much."

Queen Hemlock let out an incoherent scream of rage.

"Well," Nightshade said, tucking the shattered scepter into a hidden pocket in the costume's skirt. "Bye, Mom."

She turned to walk away.

"You can't switch allegiances *now*, you fool!" Queen Hemlock snapped. "Victory's Bloom won't ever take you back!"

Nightshade paused. Then she turned around. "True enough, after everything I said at the competition. But who said I still *want* to be part of a team?"

"You're a fool if you don't."

"No, I'm a fool if I do. I wasn't lying when I told them I quit. But I can fight perfectly well by myself. As you should know — you trained me."

"I'll make a new scepter soon!" Queen Hemlock snarled. "And then I'll come after *you!*"

Nightshade paused to consider this.

"I'm sure you will. Then I'll defeat you again. Goodbye, Mom."

She walked out the door and headed for the exit.

Queen Hemlock was left in smoldering frustration and rage.

The girl with blonde hair stepped into the bright sunlight. She paused to take a deep breath. She didn't think she'd ever gone anywhere outside the lair without her mother's express orders.

"Hmm, I think I'll enter next year's solo magical girl competition as Starlight, Princess of Determination," she mused. "I wonder if I'll stand a chance to win?"

Prancing down the hill, she headed off in a random direction. It didn't matter where she was going. Anywhere where she could be by herself would do.

From now on, her life would be her own.

www.ingramcontent.com/pod-product-compliance
Lightning Source LLC
Chambersburg PA
CBHW022043050726
47591CB00003B/932